# LA ORUGA MUY IMPACIENTE

## Ross Burach

Scholastic Inc.

5

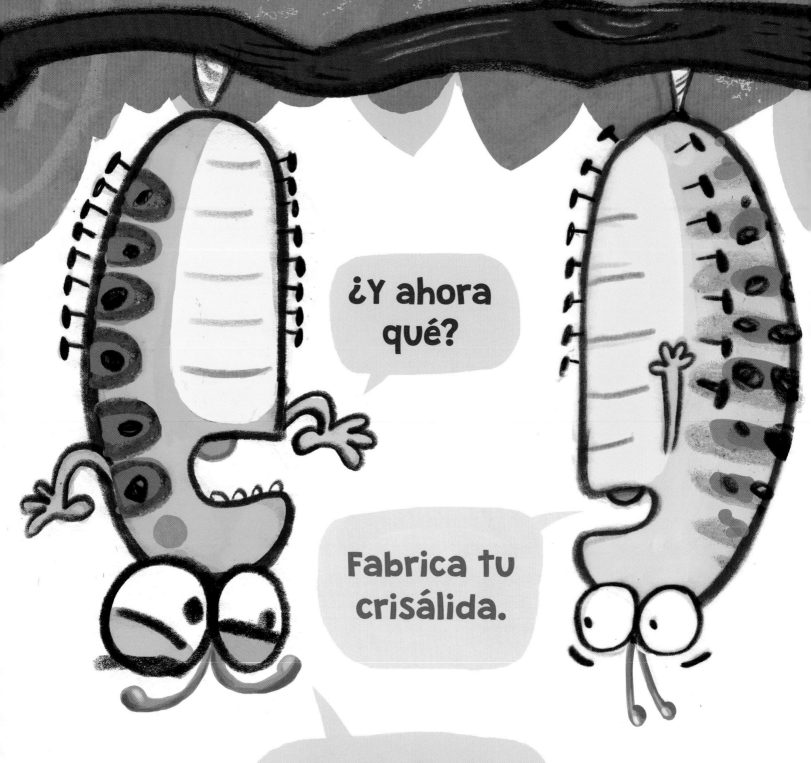

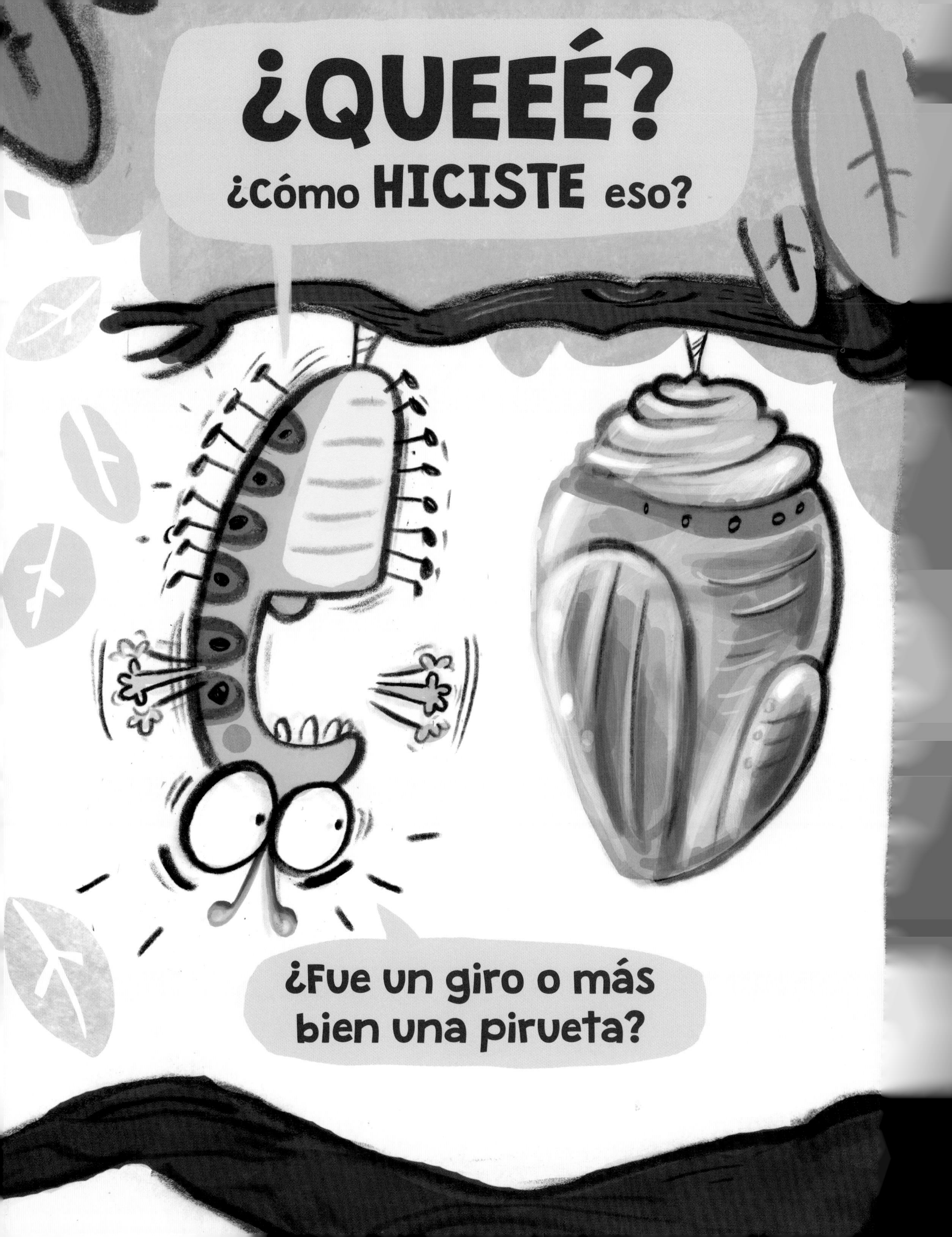
¿QUEEEÉ?
¿Cómo HICISTE eso?
¿Fue un giro o más bien una pirueta?

¿Y ahora qué?
Sé paciente y deja que la naturaleza haga su trabajo.
Paciente. Claro. Claro. Ya lo tengo.

Tengo una pregunta.

¡TODAVÍA NO!

Ni siquiera sabes lo que iba a preguntar.

Está bien. Pregunta.

¿Cómo te va? Y, de paso... ¿YA SOY UNA MARIPOSA?

¡NO! ¡SÉ PACIENTE!

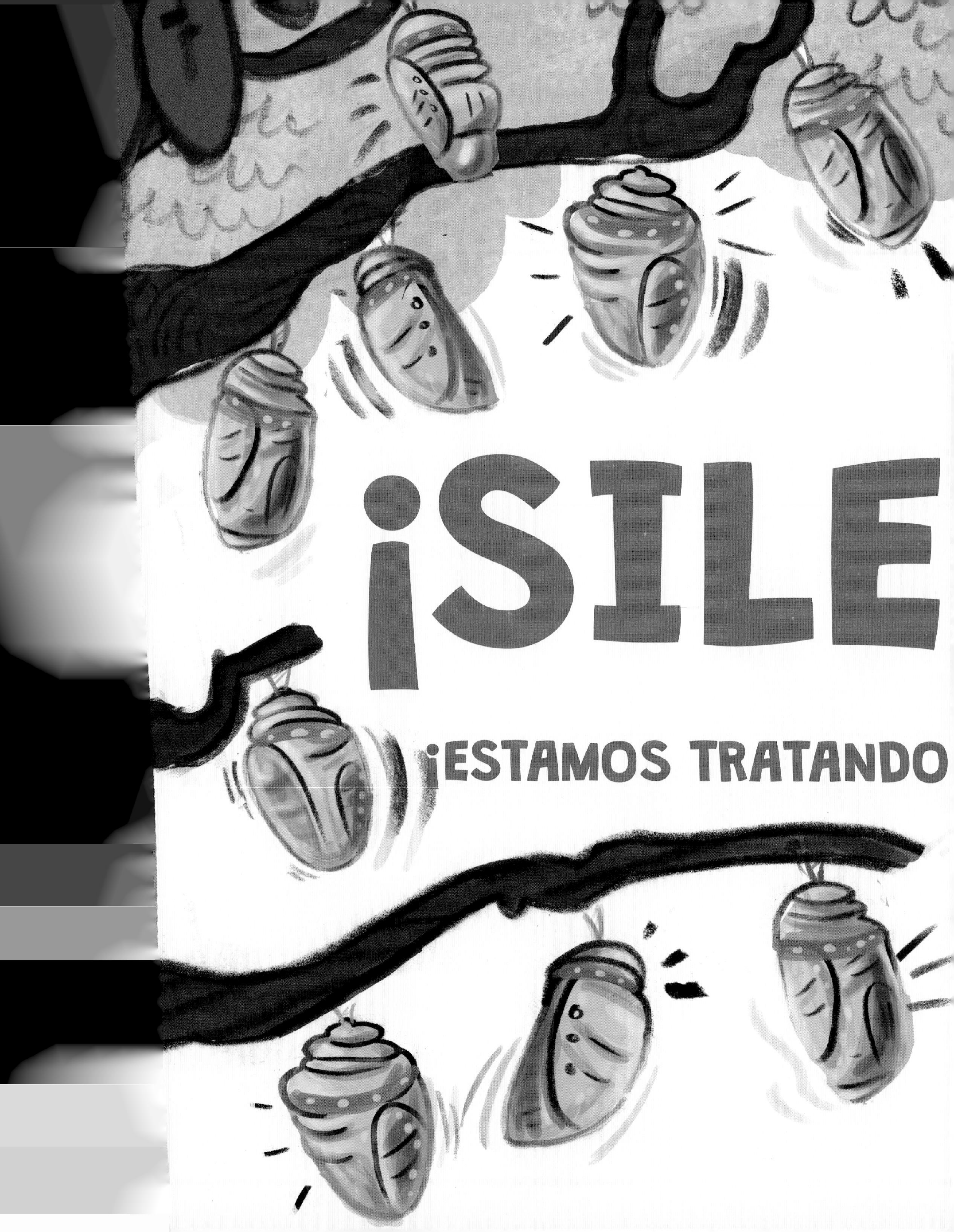

# ¡SILE

¡ESTAMOS TRATANDO

# NCIO!

## DE METAMORFOSEARNOS!

Está bien.
Está bien.

OBVIAMENTE YO LO SÉ... PERO ¿SABES cuánto tiempo demora esto?
Dos semanas.
Claro. Claro. Dos semanas.

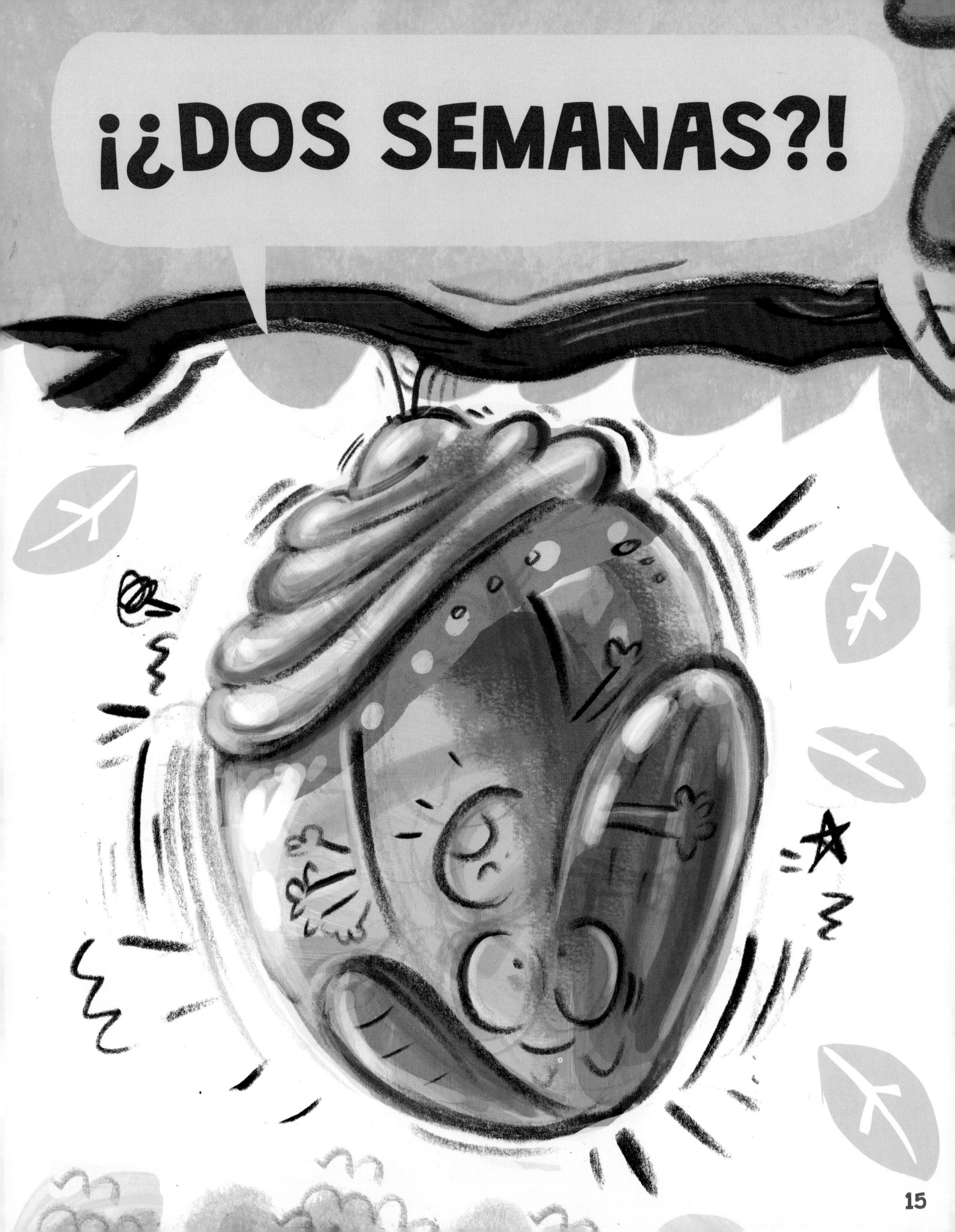
¡¿DOS SEMANAS?!

17

# Atención, mundo.
## Deléitense con la visión de esta hermosa...

# ¡¡¡ESPERA!!!

¿Dónde están mis alas?

¡SPLAT!

Hora de intentar otra cosa.

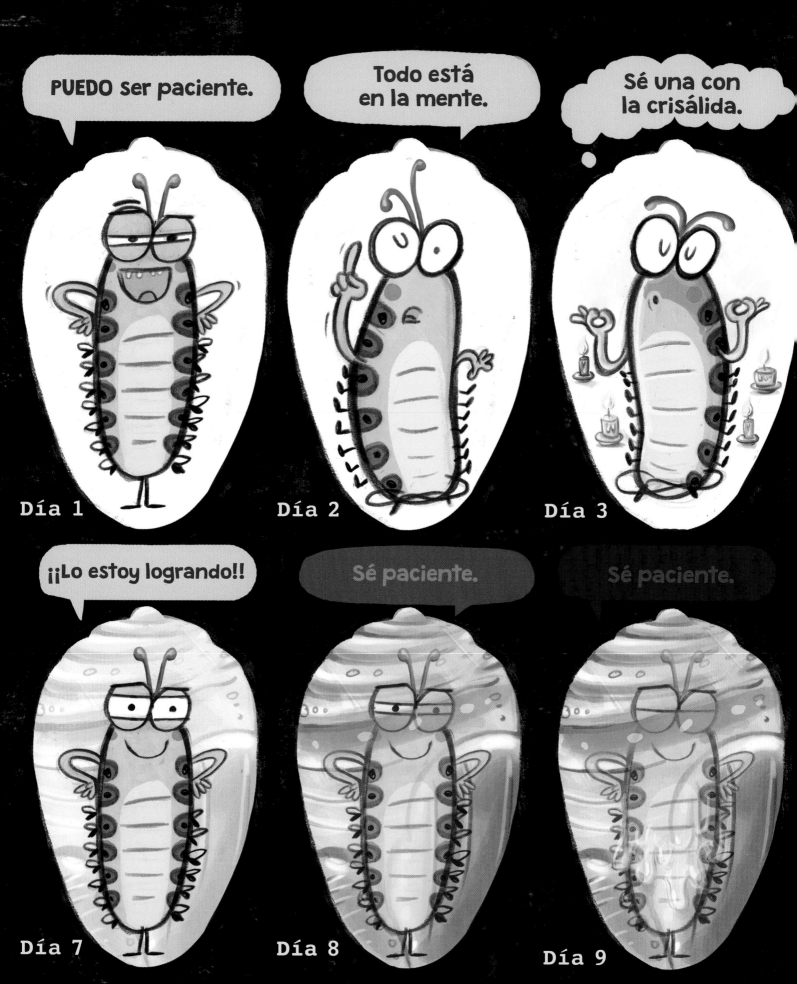

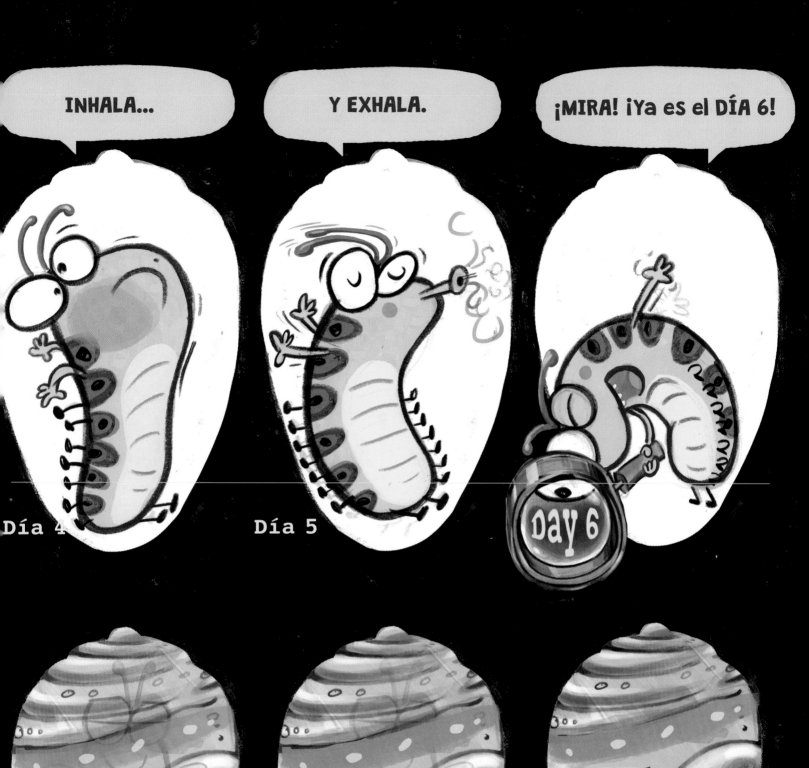

# ¡Lo logré! Soy una

# MARIPOSA

¡¿YA ESTAMOS LLEGANDO?!

Uff.

Para mamá, gracias
por ser siempre paciente.

Originally published in English as *The Very Impatient Caterpillar* · Translated by Abel Berriz · Copyright © 2019 by Ross Burach · Translation copyright © 2020 by Scholastic Inc. · All rights reserved. Published by Scholastic Inc., *Publishers Since 1920*. SCHOLASTIC, SCHOLASTIC EN ESPAÑOL, and associated logos are trademarks and/or registered trademarks of Scholastic Inc. · The publisher does not have any control over and does not assume any responsibility for author or third-party websites or their content. · No part of this publication may be reproduced, stored in a retrieval system, or transmitted in any form or by any means, electronic, mechanical, photocopying, recording, or otherwise, without written permission of the publisher. For information regarding permission, write to Scholastic Inc., Attention: Permissions Department, 557 Broadway, New York, NY 10012. · This book is a work of fiction. Names, characters, places, and incidents are either the product of the author's imagination or are used fictitiously, and any resemblance to actual persons living or dead, business establishments, events, or locales is entirely coincidental. · ISBN 978-1-338-60113-8 · 4 5 6 7 8 9 10 11 12   40   29 28 27 26 25 24 23 22 21   · Printed in U.S.A.   32 · First Spanish printing 202 Ross Burach's art was created with pencil, crayon, acrylic paint, and digital coloring. · The text type was set in Grandstander Classic Bold. The display type was set in Grandstander Classic Bold. The book was printed on 157 gsm Lumisilk Matt Art Paper and bound at Tien-Wah Press. · Production was overseen by Nora Milman. · Manufacturing was supervised by Faith Sagaille. The book was art directed by Marijka Kostiw, designed by Ross Burach and Marijka Kostiw. Original edition edited by Tracy Mack.

Scholastic Inc., 557 Broadway, New York, NY 10012